The Sporty Fairies

For Aphra O'Brien

Special thanks to
Sue Mongredien

ORCHARD BOOKS
338 Euston Road, London NW1 3BH
Orchard Books Australia
Level 17/207 Kent Street, Sydney, NSW 2000
A Paperback Original

First published in 2008 by Orchard Books.

HiT entertainment

© 2008 Rainbow Magic Limited.
A HIT Entertainment company. Rainbow Magic
is a trademark of Rainbow Magic Limited.
Reg. U.S. Pat. & Tm. Off. And other countries.

Illustrations © Orchard Books 2008

A CIP catalogue record for this book is available
from the British Library.

ISBN 978 1 84616 890 1
1 3 5 7 9 10 8 6 4 2

Printed in Great Britain

Orchard Books is a division of Hachette Children's Books,
an Hachette Livre UK company

www.orchardbooks.co.uk

Zoe
the Skating
Fairy

by Daisy Meadows

ORCHARD BOOKS

www.rainbowmagic.co.uk

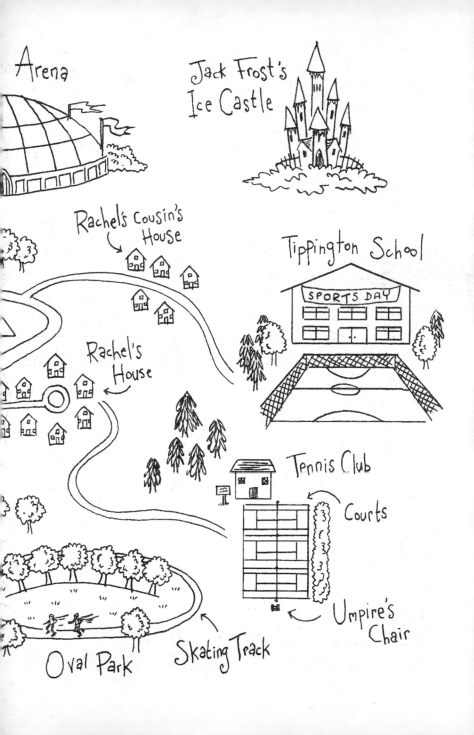

The Fairyland Olympics are about to start,
And my crafty goblins are going to take part.
We'll win this year, for I've got a cunning plan.
I'm sending my goblins to the arena in Fairyland.

The Magic Sporty Objects that make sports safe and fun,
Will be stolen by my goblins, to keep until we've won.
Sporty Fairies, prepare to lose and to watch us win.
Goblins, follow my commands, and let the games begin!

Contents

Skating Struggles

Rachel Walker held on tightly to the
park railings as she stood up on her
in-line skates. "Whoa-a-a!" she laughed,
as her feet moved slightly in different
directions. "How are you getting
on, Kirsty?"

Kirsty Tate, Rachel's best friend, was
still sitting on the grass, tying the laces

on her skates. She fastened the top straps,
then smiled up at Rachel. Kirsty was
staying with Rachel's family for a week
during the Easter holidays, and today
the girls had come to Oval Park, near
the Walkers' house.

"All right…I think," Kirsty replied,
clutching Rachel's hand and standing up.
Then she grinned. "We must be mad to
be skating today after everything that's
happened to the Sporty Fairies," she said,
wobbling on her wheels.

"At least we're well-protected," Rachel reminded her, tapping on Kirsty's helmet. "And this is such a good place to skate, I'm sure we'll still have fun."

The girls certainly were well-protected – with helmets, knee pads and elbow pads, just in case either of them took a tumble. And Rachel was right, the park was perfect for skating, with its wide path looping around the edge, where lots of skaters and skateboarders were trying out their skills. It was a warm sunny day, with a fresh breeze just rustling through the leaves in the trees, and making the daffodils nod their yellow heads.

Unfortunately, there seemed to be a lot of bumps and falls taking place amongst the skaters today. Kirsty and

Rachel watched as a boy on
a skateboard tried to do a jump,
mis-timed it, and fell off
his board onto the
grass nearby. He
got up, unhurt
but looking
puzzled. "Why
isn't that jump
working today?"
they heard him
mutter to himself.

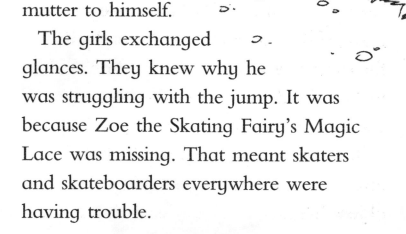

The girls exchanged
glances. They knew why he
was struggling with the jump. It was
because Zoe the Skating Fairy's Magic
Lace was missing. That meant skaters
and skateboarders everywhere were
having trouble.

Nobody else knew it – not even their parents – but Rachel and Kirsty had a wonderful secret. They were friends with the fairies, and had helped them out many times. This time, they had been called to Fairyland by King Oberon and Queen Titania, who'd asked them to help the Sporty Fairies find their Magic Sporty Objects. When the Magic Sporty Objects were in their proper places – either with their fairy keepers, or in their lockers – they ensured that sports were fun and safe for everyone in the human world and in Fairyland. But when the objects weren't where they were supposed to be, their magic only worked on anyone who was very near the object itself.

The Fairyland Olympics were due to be held soon, and Jack Frost was desperate to win the prize — a golden cup full of luck. That was why he'd ordered his goblins to steal the Magic Sporty Objects from the fairies' lockers. He wanted his goblin team to win all the events, and get the prize.

While the Sporty Fairies were without their special objects, things were going wrong in sports all over the world. Kirsty and Rachel had already helped find Helena the Horseriding Fairy's Magic Hard Hat and Francesca the Football Fairy's Magic Football. But there were still five Magic Sporty Objects missing.

"I hope we find Zoe's Magic Lace soon," Rachel said, as she stepped shakily onto the path and took a step forwards.

"I don't feel very confident on these skates today."

Kirsty nodded. "Nor me," she replied. "But remember what the Fairy Queen always says: we mustn't go looking for fairy magic; it will find us!"

The girls set off along the path, leaning forward and swinging their arms to help them skate faster. It was hard work, though, and they kept losing their balance.

"I know I'm usually better at skating than this," Kirsty sighed as she wobbled around a corner.

Whoosh! Just then, four young skaters, wearing identical tracksuits and in-line skates, zipped past the girls at an amazing speed. Rachel and Kirsty almost fell over in surprise.

Rachel stared after them. "Well, they seem to be doing all right," she remarked.

The girls watched the group of skaters, who had now moved into a diamond formation. They looked like young boys but then, as the one at the front turned to call something to the one at the back, Kirsty noticed that he had a greenish tint to his skin.

"They're goblins!" Kirsty gasped.

Rachel nodded. "Yes," she said, "and since they're all skating so well, I bet they've got Zoe's Magic Lace with them!"

An Unexpected Shower

"After them!" cried Kirsty, and she and Rachel did their best to skate faster after the four goblins, but it was no good. The girls were just too slow and shaky, and they could see that there was no way they were going to be able to catch up with the speedy skaters.

"What can we do?" Rachel said helplessly. "The goblins are already way ahead of us."

"And, look, the path bends through the trees further along," Kirsty pointed out. "They'll be out of sight soon."

The girls rolled to a stop by a tree, both feeling rather hopeless as the goblins shot off into the distance.

"Shall we take off our skates and run?" Rachel suggested. "We'd be quicker then."

"We still wouldn't be as quick as the goblins," Kirsty replied. "They're just flying along." She sighed. "If only we had fairy wings and could really fly!" she added. "Then we'd be able to catch up with them."

Just then, the girls heard a peal of silvery laughter above their heads, and they spotted Zoe the Skating Fairy zipping out of the tree to hover in the air in front of them! The girls had already met Zoe, and all the other Sporty Fairies, when they'd first started their adventure.

21

They were delighted to see her again.
Zoe had long red hair, and wore
a funky cropped top and skating shorts.
A pretty blue pendant hung around
her neck, sparkling in the sunshine.

"Did someone say they'd like some
fairy wings?" she asked, smiling and
twirling her wand between her fingers.
"I can help with that."

"Oh, thank you," Rachel said
eagerly. "We've spotted four goblins on
skates, Zoe, and we're sure they've got
your Magic Lace because they're
skating brilliantly!"

"Unlike everyone else here today,"
Kirsty added, as a girl on rollerskates
veered off the path nearby, just missing
a large bush.

Zoe winced as the girl fell over onto

the grass. Luckily, she was wearing a helmet and wasn't hurt. "Oops!" Zoe said. "I see what you mean, girls. Come behind this tree, out of sight, and I'll turn you into fairies."

Kirsty and Rachel did as she asked, and Zoe waved her wand over them. Immediately, a shower of sparkling fairy dust surrounded the girls and transformed them into fairies.

Rachel fluttered her wings in delight. "Come on!" she cried. "Let's catch up with those goblins."

"Fly high," Zoe reminded the girls. "We don't want anyone in the park to spot us."

The three fairies zoomed through the air until they caught sight of the four goblins down below.

"They're lining themselves up," Kirsty noticed. "What are they doing?"

Rachel stared. The goblins had split up, so that each one was the same distance away from the next. "Is it some kind of trap?" she wondered nervously.

The friends watched as the goblin at the back of the line began skating along the path towards his friend. "He's got my Magic Lace!" Zoe exclaimed, pointing at a shimmering object in his hand. "What's he doing with it?"

As the goblin reached his friend, he handed the lace over. Then the second goblin skated off, while the first goblin stopped and watched him go.

"They're practising for a relay race," Kirsty realised.

"And using the Magic Lace as a baton!" Rachel added.

Up ahead, the fairies could see that
a third goblin was
waiting in position,
near a copse of
oak trees. Seeing
the oak trees gave
Rachel an idea.

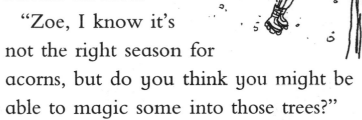

"Zoe, I know it's
not the right season for
acorns, but do you think you might be
able to magic some into those trees?"

"Yes, no problem," Zoe replied,
"but why?"

"If we can get to the trees before the
third goblin starts his part of the race,"
Rachel explained, "we can shower him
with magic acorns, and then, while
he's distracted, swoop down and grab
the lace!"

"That's a great idea!" Kirsty cried. "We'd better hurry, though; the second goblin will reach the third soon."

The three fairies sped along as fast as they could. Zoe pointed her wand at the trees, and Rachel and Kirsty smiled as they saw hundreds of sparkling fairy acorns appear amidst the leaves.

Meanwhile, down below, the second
goblin had handed the lace on.
The third goblin promptly set off on
his skates, through the trees, clutching
the Magic Lace. As he did so,
Zoe waved her wand again and
the branches began to shake.
Soon, lots and lots of glittering
green acorns were showering down
around the third goblin.

Kirsty's Sweet Idea

"Help!" yelled the goblin, covering his head with his hands. "What's happening?"

"There's the lace!" Zoe hissed, spotting it between his fingers. "If I use my magic to keep the branches still, will you two try to get it?"

"Of course," Kirsty replied eagerly.

Zoe touched her wand to the branch
in front of her, and all the trees stopped
showering acorns and became still. Kirsty
and Rachel immediately swooped down
towards the goblin's hand.

Unfortunately, now that the acorns
had stopped falling, the goblin had
uncovered his head and was staring up
at the tree. He soon caught sight of
Kirsty and Rachel speeding towards him.

"Where did you come from?" he
cried, trying to skate away from them.

But there were
so many acorns
littering the ground
that the wheels of
one skate jammed
and the goblin lost
his balance. His
arms flailed and
the sparkling lace
fell from his grip and
dropped to the ground.

Rachel's eyes lit up as she saw it fall,
and she plunged towards it. Her fingers
were just about to fold around the
Magic Lace when the goblin's
big bottom thundered to the ground,
trapping the lace underneath it.

Rachel and Kirsty only just managed to dart out of the way in time to avoid being squashed. They looked despairingly at the fallen-down goblin, and then at each other. There was no way they could get the Magic Lace now that the goblin was sitting on it.

The goblin picked himself up and grabbed hold of the lace once more. Then he stuck his tongue out at the fairies. "Keep your sparkly acorns to yourself!" he snapped. "You're not getting the Magic Lace, and that's that!" Then, picking his way carefully through the acorns, he skated off towards the fourth goblin, further down the path.

Zoe put her hands on her hips. "Oh, we so nearly had it!" she sighed. "Well, we'll just have to make a new plan."

Rachel and Kirsty nodded and, together, the three friends flew after the goblin. They caught up to see that the relay had now finished, and the four goblins were shouting at each other. The friends perched on a branch to listen.

"If you can't go faster than that, you'll be dropped from the team!" the first goblin scolded the third.

"If you skate like that in the Fairyland Olympics, we'll lose," the second goblin added. "Jack Frost will be furious!"

"It wasn't my fault," the third goblin argued. "I was attacked!"

"Attacked?" scoffed the fourth goblin. "By what?"

"By...an army!" the third goblin declared. "An army of fairies. They bombarded me with magic acorns!"

"Tiny little acorns?" the first goblin sneered. "So what?"

"No, no," the third goblin protested. "Not tiny little acorns. Great enormous acorns. Acorns the size of footballs!"

Kirsty and Rachel tried not to laugh out loud as the goblin's story got wilder and wilder.

"They came at me from all angles," he went on dramatically. "I could have been squashed at any moment!"

The other goblins were wide-eyed. "Ooh, squashed!" the second one repeated, glancing around nervously.

The third goblin nodded. "I was lucky to escape with my life," he boasted. "I had to fight heroically to save the Magic Lace."

"Good work," the first goblin said, clapping him on the back. "How did you keep it safe?"

The third goblin hesitated. "Um..." he began.

Rachel, Kirsty and Zoe smiled at each other. He didn't want to admit that he'd kept the lace safe by sitting on it!

"I...I just managed to keep it out of their way," he replied at last.

Just then, a voice shouted from across the park, "Doughnuts! Come and get your lovely doughnuts! Free samples! Try before you buy!"

The girls looked round to see a man setting up a doughnut stall nearby. The goblins saw it too.

"Oooh, doughnuts," the fourth goblin said, licking his lips. "I'm hungry!"

The first goblin shook his head. "We don't have time for doughnuts," he said sternly. "We need to keep practising. And we're meant to be eating healthy food before the Olympics, not cakes!" He ignored the fourth goblin's dismayed look and began issuing orders. "So, we'll do the same practice run again, ending at this tree, OK?" He pointed to a stout oak by the side of the path. "As before, once you've completed your part of the race, come back here for a time-check. Now, everyone get in position!"

With a last longing look at
the doughnut stall, the fourth goblin
trudged back to his position. So did
the others.

Kirsty looked thoughtfully at
the hungry goblin. *Just how much does
he want a doughnut?* she wondered.
Enough to fall for a trick?

Trick or Treat?

"I've got an idea," Kirsty whispered
to her friends. "Zoe, do you think that
you could make me look like a goblin?"

Zoe looked at Kirsty thoughtfully.
"I think so," she replied. "I'd just have
to turn your clothes into a tracksuit,
make you the right height and tint
your skin green." She wrinkled her nose.

"If the goblins look closely at you, they'll be able to see you're not a real goblin, though."

"If my plan works, that won't matter," Kirsty replied.

"What *is* your plan?" Rachel asked curiously.

"Well, we need to get that hungry goblin to leave his spot on the race track. Then I'll take his place," Kirsty explained, "and when the third goblin skates up and hands over the Magic Lace, I'll skate away with it!"

"Brilliant!" Zoe cried. "And the lace's powers will mean you can whizz off super-fast!" she added.

"But how will we persuade the goblin to leave the track?" Rachel asked.

The doughnut man began shouting again and Kirsty grinned.

"If you have a doughnut, Rachel, and tempt the goblin with it, he might go to the doughnut seller and get one for himself," she said. "And then Zoe can make me look like a goblin and I'll stand in his place, ready to get the lace."

Zoe beamed. "One doughnut coming up!" she cried, waving her wand. With a fizz of fairy dust, Rachel grew to her usual size, and a warm, sugary doughnut appeared in mid-air. It hovered there for a moment, then drifted into Rachel's hand.

"Ooh, pleased to eat you," Rachel said, with a giggle. The doughnut did smell delicious. Then she winked at her friends. "Here I go!"

Rachel carefully climbed down the tree, and strode towards the goblin, waving the doughnut so that its yummy scent drifted under his nose. Then she took a bite. "Mmm-mmm!" she said loudly.

The goblin stared at her and licked his lips.

"This is soooo delicious," Rachel went on, taking another nibble.

The goblin glared. "Go away!" he snapped. "I'm trying to concentrate on the relay and you're putting me off."

"Sorry," Rachel said innocently. "It's just that this doughnut is scrumptious."

The goblin watched her take another bite, then a sly look crossed his face. Suddenly, he flung out an arm to try to grab the doughnut. Rachel darted out of the way.

"Give me that!" the goblin ordered greedily.

"Get one for yourself," Rachel replied.

"The man over there is giving out free samples."

The goblin glanced over his shoulder longingly, but then his face fell. "It's my turn to race soon," he said. "I'd better not."

"Oh, you've got plenty of time," Rachel told him. "Better not wait too long, though. The doughnut man may not have very many left…"

The goblin looked panicked at the thought of missing out on a sweet treat altogether, and with a last look at Rachel's delicious doughnut, he skated off at once.

Rachel looked up at Kirsty and Zoe as they flew down to the ground.

"It's goblin time for you!" Zoe said to Kirsty, and waved her wand.

Kirsty Races Into Trouble

Sparkly red fairy dust streamed around Kirsty. She tingled all over, then felt herself getting bigger and bigger. Soon she was about half her human size, and she looked down to see that she was now wearing a tracksuit and her hands had turned green.

"Wow!" Rachel said. "You really do look a bit like a goblin."

"Not as sneaky as a real one, though," Zoe reassured her.

"I'll go and wait in the fourth goblin's position on the track," Kirsty said.

"OK," Zoe replied. "We'll meet you by the oak tree that marks the finishing line. Good luck!"

Kirsty stepped onto the path and checked over her shoulder to see where the third goblin in the relay was. He was skating right towards her, so she whipped her head back again. She didn't want him to get a proper look at her face. Her heart pounded with excitement. She hoped her plan was going to work.

She could hear the third goblin's skates now as he drew nearer, so Kirsty slowly began skating herself, her hand stretched out behind her ready to take the lace.

53

Then, just as she felt the third goblin putting the Magic Lace into her palm, she heard an indignant voice cry, "Hey! It's my turn!"

Kirsty turned and saw that the fourth goblin had returned, munching his doughnut and looking astonished to see her in his place. Kirsty could think of only one thing to do: she grabbed the lace from the third goblin and took off at top speed before either of the goblins could reach her.

"What's going on?" she heard
the fourth goblin yell as she sped away.
Meanwhile, Zoe had transformed
Rachel back into a fairy and they had
zoomed to the finishing line, watching
everything from above. They saw
the third and fourth goblins stare at
each other, and then at Kirsty, who
was now whizzing away. Then they
saw it dawn on the goblins that Kirsty
wasn't actually a goblin at all.

"We've been tricked!" the goblin with
the doughnut shouted
furiously. "It was all
your fault, giving
her the Magic
Lace like that!
Couldn't you see it wasn't me?"

"It wasn't my fault!" the third goblin
retorted. "If you'd stayed in position,
like you were supposed to do, none
of this would have happened!"

"Well, we need to catch her,"
the goblin with the doughnut said.
"Right now!"

The two goblins began skating after
Kirsty. Now that they no longer had
the Magic Lace, they couldn't go
as quickly as before, but they kept on
skating, puffing and panting as they went.

Then Rachel noticed that the two goblins who had skated the first part of the relay had doubled back on themselves. They were now making their way towards the finishing line, too, but from the opposite direction. Suddenly, she saw one of them nudge the other and point ahead at Kirsty, who was zooming towards them.

"Oh, no!" Rachel cried. "The other two goblins have spotted Kirsty!"

Rachel and Zoe immediately set off towards Kirsty, too. The two goblins who had been first in the relay seemed to have guessed something was wrong, because they suddenly started skating much faster.

"They're going to try to head Kirsty off!" Zoe realised.

"Poor Kirsty," Rachel cried in horror. "She'll be caught in the middle of all four goblins!"

Rachel and Zoe flew towards Kirsty as fast as they could.

"I'll turn Kirsty into a fairy," Zoe
decided. "Then she can fly up into
the air, away from the goblins."

"What about the lace?" Rachel
reminded her. "It might be too heavy
for her to carry when she's a fairy."

Zoe shook her
head. "Don't
worry," she said.
"The Magic
Sporty Objects
change their size
according to who's
holding them. When Kirsty becomes
a fairy, the lace will magically become
its Fairyland size." Then she frowned
anxiously and flapped her wings harder.
"But we need to get to Kirsty before
the goblins do…"

Rachel nodded. They had to get to Kirsty in time, otherwise her friend would be at the mercy of four goblins!

Flying High

Down on the track, Kirsty glanced
over her shoulder to see that
the two goblins were still behind
her, glaring as they gave chase.
But when she looked ahead again,
she gasped in shock. Skating
straight towards her were the
first and second goblins.

Kirsty looked all around, but there was no way out. She couldn't skate off the path and onto the grass, because there was a fenced-off tennis court on one side of her and flowerbeds on the other. She was trapped!

The goblins were closing in and Kirsty felt sick with fright. They were so close now that she could hear them shouting at her to give back the lace.

Their arms were outstretched,
reaching for the Magic Sporty Object.

"Help!" Kirsty cried, wondering where
Zoe and Rachel were, and hoping they
would hear her. "Help!"

And then, at the
very last second,
just as one of the
goblins was
about to seize
the Magic
Lace, she saw
a cloud of
bright sparkles
swirl around
her, and felt
herself shrinking
down and down
and down...

Oh, what a relief it was to feel wings on her back and find that she was a fairy once more! Kirsty zipped up into the air, flapping her wings as hard as she could, as the goblins below jumped up and down, trying to grab her.

"Kirsty, are you OK?" Rachel cried, as she and Zoe flew over, panting.

"Yes," Kirsty replied faintly. "That was close, though. Thanks, Zoe!"

The three fairies landed on a branch of a nearby oak tree to get their breath back. Instantly, the goblins tried to climb the tree. They still had their skates on,

though, so they were finding it
a struggle.

Zoe put her hands on her hips and
shouted down to them. "Any more
trouble from you lot and I really will
make magic acorns the size of footballs
to drop on you!" she warned. "And
then you'll be goblin pancakes!"

The goblins hesitated. "I don't want to be a goblin pancake!" wailed one, dropping down from the tree trunk.

"Nor me," chorused the others, stumbling away from the oak. Soon, the four of them were skating away as fast as they could.

Kirsty handed Zoe the Magic Lace, smiling.

Zoe looked delighted to have it back. "Thank you so much!" she breathed. She touched her wand to the lace and a flash of bright red sparkles surrounded it. "There," she said happily. "Now all will be well again with skaters everywhere."

The three of them flew down to the ground, and Zoe waved her wand over Kirsty and Rachel, magically turning them back to their normal size.

"Thanks again, girls," she said. "Enjoy the rest of your time in the park. You'll find skating much more fun now, I promise."

"Thanks, Zoe," Rachel replied. "It was great helping you. Goodbye!"

"Goodbye," Kirsty added.

"Bye, girls," Zoe said, and, with a burst of red fairy dust that sparkled for a second in the air, she was gone.

Rachel nudged Kirsty as a group of boys went by on in-line skates, whooping as they carried out some tricky-looking turns. "Look, everyone's skating well again," she said.

Rachel was right. Nobody was falling over any more. All the skaters and skateboarders looked as if they were enjoying themselves as they whizzed along.

Kirsty grinned. "I bet we'll be able to skate better now, too," she said happily. "Come on, let's find out. I'll race you to that tree!"

And the two friends skated off together, laughing as they went.

Another Magic Sporty Object was safely back with its fairy keeper – now there were just four left to find!

RAINBOW magic

The Sporty Fairies

Rachel and Kirsty must now help

Naomi the Netball Fairy

Naomi has had her Magic Netball
stolen by the pesky goblins! Can Rachel
and Kirsty help her to get it back
so that netball can be fun again
for everyone?

Spring into Sport

"What shall we do after lunch, Kirsty?"
asked Rachel Walker, as she finished
her apple.

Kirsty Tate, Rachel's best friend, grinned.
"You know what I'd really like to do?"
she replied. "I'd like to find Naomi the
Netball Fairy's Magic Netball!"

Rachel and Kirsty shared a very special
secret. While holidaying on Rainspell
Island, the two girls had become friends
with the fairies, and now Rachel and
Kirsty always helped out whenever there
was a problem in Fairyland.

"Remember what Queen Titania told

us," Rachel reminded Kirsty. "We have
to let the magic come to us."

"I know, but I'm feeling really
impatient today," Kirsty replied. "If we
don't find all the Magic Sporty Objects
before I go home in a few days' time,
Jack Frost and his goblins will win
the Fairyland Olympics Cup!"

The Fairyland Olympics were due
to take place at the end of the week,
but mean Jack Frost had stolen the
Sporty Fairies' seven Magic Sporty
Objects. These magical objects made sure
that sport was fun and exciting, as well
as played fairly, in both the human world
and Fairyland. But Jack Frost wanted
his goblin servants to cheat their way to
victory in the Fairyland Olympics, using
the magic of the Sporty Objects to win

every single event. He had sent the goblins into the human world to keep the magic objects hidden away and to practise their sports. But Rachel and Kirsty had promised the Sporty Fairies that they would try to get the seven objects back before the fairy games began.

Rachel sighed. "The missing objects mean that sports in our world are affected too," she added. "I wonder how many netball games are going wrong right now because Naomi's Magic Netball is missing..."

Read the rest of

Naomi the Netball Fairy

to find out what magic happens next...

Have you ever wanted to name
your own Rainbow Magic Fairy?

Now is your chance to help us choose
the most magical, sparkly name
for a Rainbow Magic Fairy!*

Log on to www.rainbowmagic.co.uk
to unlock the magic within!

www.rainbowmagic.co.uk is the place to
go for games, downloads, competitions,
activities, latest news, and lots of fun!

Plus meet the fairies and find out
about their amazing adventures
with Rachel and Kirsty.

* Competition runs from April 2008 for four weeks –
please see www.rainbowmagic.co.uk for more details
For terms and conditions please see www.hachettechildrens.co.uk/terms

Win Rainbow Magic goodies!

In every book in the Rainbow Magic Sporty Fairies series
(books 57–63) there is a hidden picture of a hoop with a secret letter
in it. Find all seven letters and re-arrange them to make
a special Sporty Fairies word, then send it to us. Each month we
will put the entries into a draw and select one winner to receive
a Rainbow Magic Sparkly T-shirt and Goody Bag!

Send your entry on a postcard to Rainbow Magic Sporty Fairies
Competition, Orchard Books, 338 Euston Road, London NW1 3BH.
Australian readers should write to Hachette Children's Books,
Level 17/207 Kent Street, Sydney, NSW 2000.
New Zealand readers should write to Rainbow Magic Competition,
4 Whetu Place, Mairangi Bay, Auckland, NZ. Don't forget to
include your name and address. Only one entry per child.
Final draw: 30th April 2009.

Good luck!

Look out for the Music Fairies!

POPPY
THE PIANO FAIRY
978-1-40830-033-6

ELLIE
THE GUITAR FAIRY
978-1-40830-030-5

FIONA
THE FLUTE FAIRY
978-1-40830-029-9

DANNI
THE DRUM FAIRY
978-1-40830-028-2

MAYA
THE HARP FAIRY
978-1-40830-031-2

VICTORIA
THE VIOLIN FAIRY
978-1-40830-027-5

SADIE
THE SAXOPHONE FAIRY
978-1-40830-032-9

Available September 2008